Po-Tolo
Plan Bee From Outer Space

'For Con and Em ...'

TOP THAT

Licensed exclusively to Top That Publishing Ltd
Tide Mill Way, Woodbridge, Suffolk, IP12 1AP, UK
www.topthatpublishing.com
Copyright © 2014 Christian Oliver
All rights reserved
0 2 4 6 8 9 7 5 3 1
Manufactured in China

Written and ilustrated by Christian Oliver

ISBN 978-1-78445-376-3

A catalogue record for this book is available from the British Library

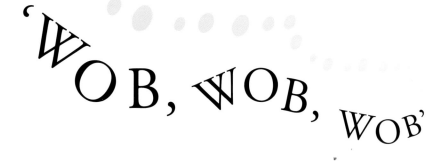 

'WOB, WOB, WOB'

A spaceman named Po-Tolo came to Earth
one day in a spaceship called Nommo.

His world was in trouble and he
was looking for help.

Flying through the garden, a busy bumblebee, named Izzy, bumped into Po-Tolo and his friend (a purple octopus called Lop).

'Hello,' said Po-Tolo. 'Can you help us?'

'Me? Help you?' Izzy sniffed. 'I'm only a little bumblebee. I couldn't possibly help.'

'You don't have to be big to be a big help!' replied Po-Tolo. 'On our world the bees have all disappeared and all of the plants are dying. We need bees to save our planet. Will any of your bee friends come back with us?'

'We're dying too!' said Izzy.

'We don't know why, but we're dropping like flies!'

'Hey! Don't be rude!' cried a fly who
was passing by.

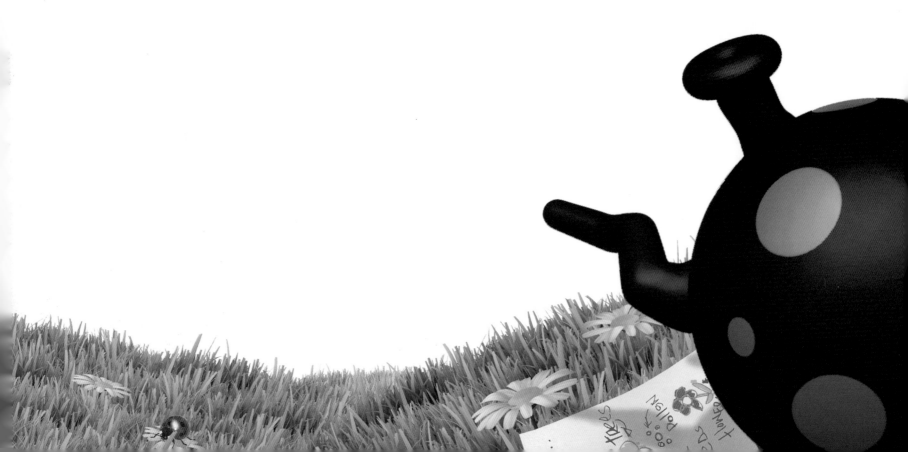

Fzzzzzzzzzzz!

'HEY!'

After looking at Po-Tolo and Lop's plan, Izzy decided to fly back to the nest to ask the queen bee if they could help Po-Tolo.

'Wait here!' she said, before buzzing off.

While Po-Tolo and Lop waited for Izzy to return, something flew over their heads.

'Another bee!' shouted Lop.
'See if he can help too.'

Po-Tolo leapt up and flew towards the bee. But it wasn't a bee, it was a wasp! Wasps hate to be chased, so it turned and stung poor Po-Tolo.

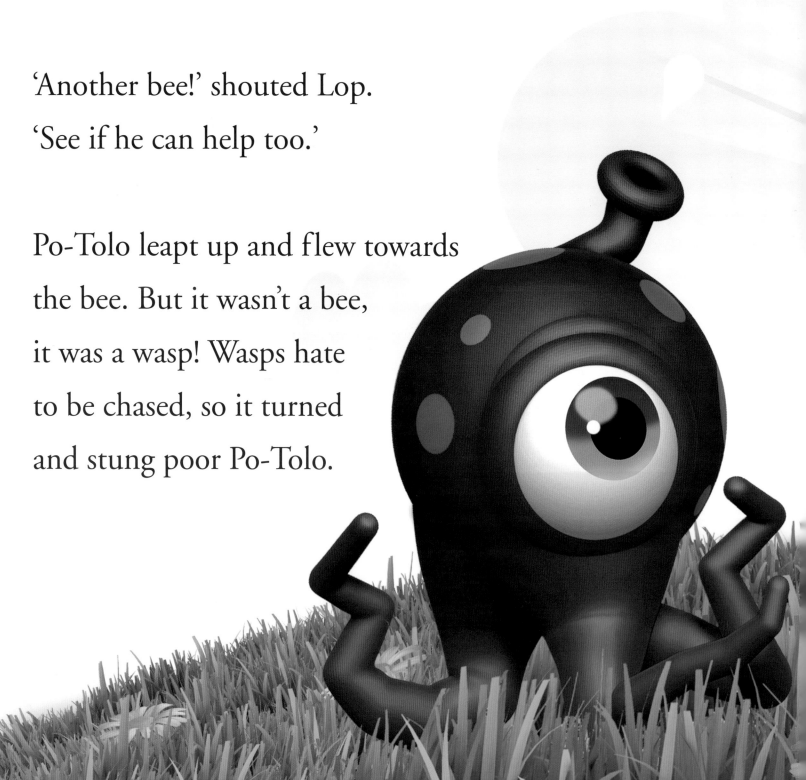

When Izzy returned, she found poor Po-Tolo deflated and Lop shrieking for help.

'Help, Izzy!' yelped Lop. 'Po-Tolo's suit has popped!'

Izzy turned and quickly flew to the garden shed to find the bicycle repair kit. Clever Izzy had a plan!

Bzzzzzzzzzzz!

Lop stopped shrieking and locked his blowhole
to the hole in Po-Tolo's suit.

PUFF... PUFF... PUFF...

Then he blew and blew
with all his might!

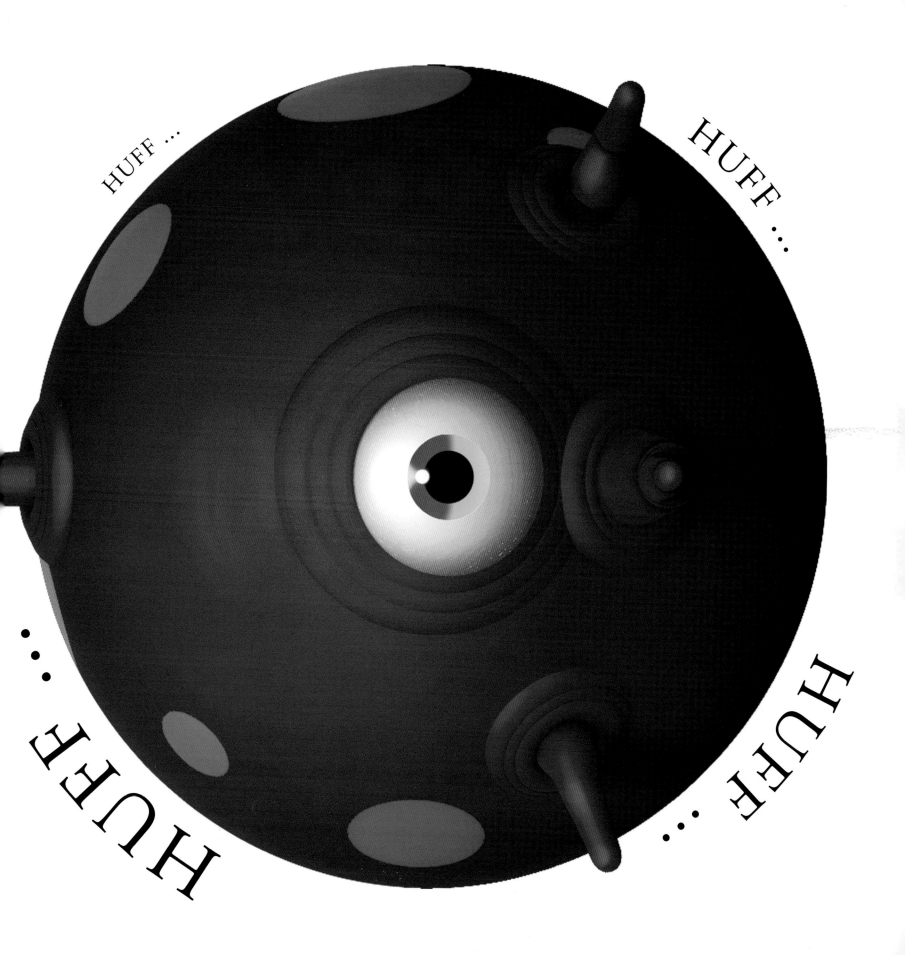

When Po-Tolo's suit was fully inflated again, Lop stopped puffing and popped one of his tentacles into the hole.

Then Izzy glued a rubber patch, from the bicycle repair kit, over the hole in Po-Tolo's suit.
It was as good as new!

'Phew!' wheezed Po-Tolo. 'Thank you!'

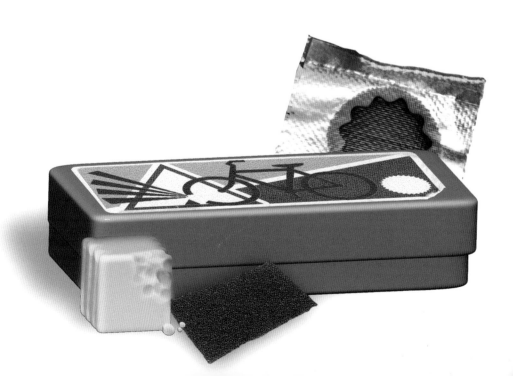

'Hooray!'

When everyone had calmed down, Po-Tolo asked if the queen bee had given permission for Earth bees to fly with him and Lop to their home planet.

'The queen bee agrees!' sneezed Izzy, excitedly. 'You have two legions of brave Earth bees at your disposal!'

'Hooray!' cried Po-Tolo and Lop together.

HUMMMMMMM!

Lop oversaw the loading of the spaceship, Nommo, while Po-Tolo had a bumblecuddle with Izzy.

Bzzzz!

Po-Tolo promised to come back to Earth soon, and then they blasted off to rescue their home planet.